This Book Belongs To

_____

Color Test Page

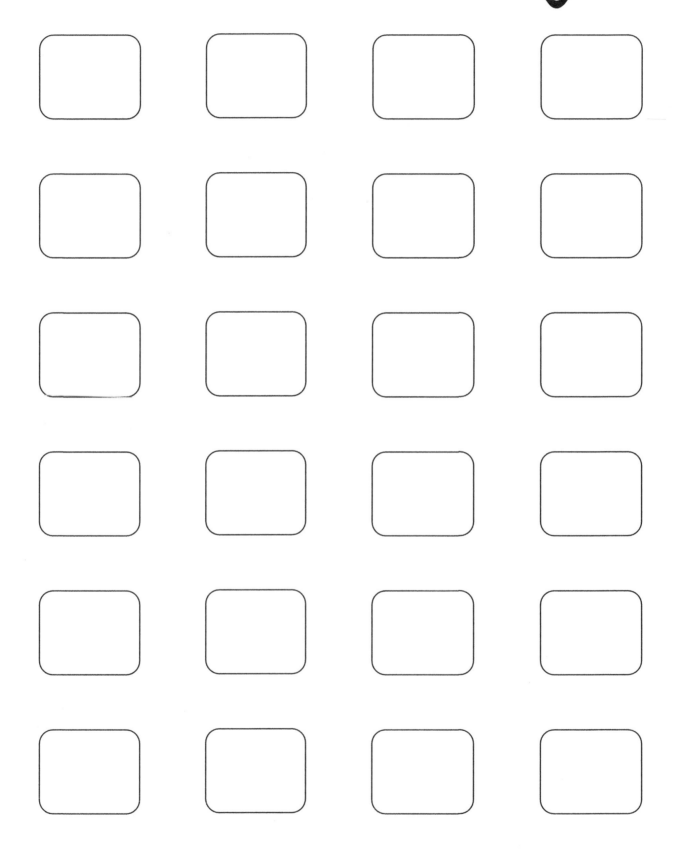

Same Illustrations

- In case of a mistake or mistakes.
- To use different color combinations.
- To let someone else color.
- To cut the designs

Made in the USA
Monee, IL
18 February 2023

28081428R00031